A Note to Parents and Caregivers:

Read-it! Readers are for children who are just starting on the amazing road to reading. These beautiful books support both the acquisition of reading skills and the love of books.

 The PURPLE LEVEL presents basic topics and objects using high frequency words and simple language patterns.

 The RED LEVEL presents familiar topics using common words and repeating sentence patterns.

 The BLUE LEVEL presents new ideas using a larger vocabulary and varied sentence structure.

 The YELLOW LEVEL presents more challenging ideas, a broad vocabulary, and wide variety in sentence structure.

 The GREEN LEVEL presents more complex ideas, an extended vocabulary range, and expanded language structures.

 The ORANGE LEVEL presents a wide range of ideas and concepts using challenging vocabulary and complex language structures.

When sharing a book with your child, read in short stretches, pausing often to talk about the pictures. Have your child turn the pages and point to the pictures and familiar words. And be sure to reread favorite stories or parts of stories.

There is no right or wrong way to share books with children. Find time to read with your child, and pass on the legacy of literacy.

Adria F. Klein, Ph.D.
Professor Emeritus
California State University
San Bernardino, California

Editor: Jill Kalz
Designer: Hilary Wacholz
Page Production: Melissa Kes
Art Director: Nathan Gassman
Associate Managing Editor: Christianne Jones
The illustrations in this book were created with watercolor and digitally.

Picture Window Books
151 Good Counsel Drive
P.O. Box 669
Mankato, MN 56002-0669
877-845-8392
www.picturewindowbooks.com

Printed in the United States of America.

All books published by Picture Window Books
are manufactured with paper containing at least
10 percent post-consumer waste.

Library of Congress Cataloging-in-Publication Data
Meister, Cari.
Robin Hood and the golden arrow / retold by Cari Meister ; illustrated by
Necdet Yilmaz.
p. cm. — (Read-it! readers: legends)
ISBN 978-1-4048-4843-6 (library binding)
1. Robin Hood (Legendary character)—Legends. [1. Robin Hood (Legendary
character)—Legends. 2. Folklore—England.] I. Yilmaz, Necdet, 1970- ill. II. Title.
PZ8.1.M498Rob 2008
398.2—dc22   2008006327

Robin Hood

and the
Golden Arrow

a retelling by Cari Meister
illustrated by Necdet Yilmaz

Special thanks to our reading adviser:

Adria F. Klein, Ph.D.
Professor Emeritus, California State University
San Bernardino, California

PiCTURE WiNDOW BOOKS
Minneapolis, Minnesota

Long ago, a man named Robin Hood lived in Sherwood Forest. Robin Hood sang songs. He hunted deer. No one shot arrows straighter than Robin Hood.

Robin Hood was a kind man. He gave money to poor people. He held big feasts. He rescued people who were in danger.

But Robin Hood was an outlaw. He and his friends, the Merry Men, stole from rich people. Robin didn't feel bad about stealing because he gave the riches away.

There was one man Robin Hood loved to trick. He was the sheriff of Nottingham. The sheriff was mean and heartless. He took people's land. He taxed people too much.

The sheriff hated Robin Hood. He wanted to catch him more than anything in the world. One day, the sheriff thought of a plan.

"Let's have a contest," he told the townspeople.
"The man who shoots the best arrow wins."

"What is the prize?" one man asked.

"A golden arrow," said the sheriff. "I am sure the outlaw Robin Hood will want to win that. When he gets to town, I will catch him!"

The sheriff laughed his evil laugh. He showed his sharp teeth.

"It will not be long now," he said. "Robin Hood will soon be mine!"

17

News about the contest spread fast.

"Let's go to town," Robin Hood said to his friends. "I love a good contest!"

But the Merry Men worried.

"We heard it's a trap, Robin," they said.
"The sheriff will catch you."

Robin Hood didn't want to be caught. But he wanted to go to the contest. He knew he could win the golden arrow.

"I have a plan," said Little John, one of the Merry Men. "We will go to the contest. But before we go, we will cover our everyday clothes with these cloaks."

Robin Hood covered his green everyday clothes with a long red cloak. He pulled the hood over his head. He looked in the stream and laughed. He did look different!

"Wise man!" Robin Hood said to Little John. "This will trick the sheriff."

Robin Hood and the Merry Men went to town. They entered the contest. They made up names and changed their voices. No one knew who they were.

Robin Hood shot arrow after arrow. He always hit the mark.

The townspeople cheered and clapped. "Hooray for the man in red!" they said.

The sheriff looked for Robin Hood.
He could not find him anywhere.

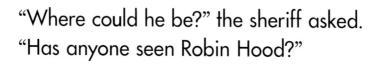

"Where could he be?" the sheriff asked.
"Has anyone seen Robin Hood?"

Of course, no one had.

27

When the contest was over, the man in red was named the winner. The sheriff gave him the golden arrow.

"Well done," the sheriff said. "You are the best shot in the land. The golden arrow belongs to you."

Robin Hood and the Merry Men laughed all the way back to Sherwood Forest. They had a great day in town.

Best of all, they tricked the sheriff once again.

More *Read-it!* Readers

Bright pictures and fun stories help you practice your reading skills. Look for more books at your level.

How Spirit Dog Made the Milky Way:
    A Retelling of a Cherokee Legend
King Arthur and the Black Knight
King Arthur and the Sword in the Stone
Mato the Bear and Devil's Tower:
    A Retelling of a Lakota Legend
Robin Hood and the Golden Arrow
Robin Hood and the Tricky Butcher

On the Web

FactHound offers a safe, fun way to find Web sites related to topics in this book. All of the sites on FactHound have been researched by our staff.

1. Visit *www.facthound.com*

2. Type in this special code:
   1404848436

3. Click on the FETCH IT button.

Your trusty FactHound will fetch the best sites for you!
A complete list of *Read-it!* Readers is available on our Web site:
www.picturewindowbooks.com